Books should be returned or renewed by the last
date above. Renew by phone **03000 41 31 31** or
online *www.kent.gov.uk/libs*

To Debbie Daniels,
for all her love and care to Audrey
and her family

Special thanks to Valerie Wilding

ORCHARD BOOKS

First published in Great Britain in 2017 by The Watts Publishing Group

1 3 5 7 9 10 8 6 4 2

Text copyright © Working Partners Ltd 2017
Illustrations copyright © Working Partners Ltd 2017
Series created by Working Partners Ltd

A CIP catalogue record for this book is available from the British Library.

ISBN 978 1 40834 414 9

Printed in Great Britain

Orchard Books
An imprint of Hachette Children's Group
Part of The Watts Publishing Group Limited
Carmelite House, 50 Victoria Embankment, London EC4Y 0DZ

An Hachette UK Company
www.hachette.co.uk
www.hachettechildrens.co.uk

Lola Fluffywhiskers Pops Up

Daisy Meadows

ORCHARD

Grizelda's Lair

Scramblepaws'
Igloo

Littleleap
Crossing
Station

Fluffywhiskers Garden
Station

Fluffywhiskers
Garden

Fluffywhiskers
Garden

Forest Halt Station

Forest Halt

Friendship
Forest

Map of Magic Mountain

Littleleap Lodge

Orchard

Mines

Heppytail Cavern

the Friendship Express

Can you keep a secret? I thought you could!

Then I'll tell you about an enchanted wood.

It lies through the door in the old oak tree,

Let's go there now - just follow me!

We'll find adventure that never ends,

And meet the Magic Animal Friends!

Love,
Goldie the Cat

Contents

CHAPTER ONE

Off to Friendship Forest!

"It's a perfect day for working outside!" said Lily Hart to her best friend Jess Forester. Her breath made little clouds in the crisp air as she raked the autumn leaves into a pile.

Jess pushed her blonde curls out of her

eyes. "And working at Helping Paw is the perfect way to spend an afternoon."

Lily's parents ran the Helping Paw Wildlife Hospital from a converted barn at the bottom of their garden. Lily and Jess loved helping out whenever they could.

Mr and Mrs Hart were inside the barn at this very moment, tending to the poorly creatures. Lily and Jess were clearing the paths between the outside runs.

Jess peered into a pen where a mother rabbit and her fluffy babies were busy

crunching on carrots. Then she swept the path in front of the aviary, a glass birdhouse full of chirping robins and swallows.

As Lily added some more leaves to the growing heap they had gathered, there was a rustling sound and some of the leaves tumbled from the pile.

"That's strange," she said. "It's not windy today."

She was just peering down to investigate the pile of leaves when she saw something out of the corner of her eye.

A cat with golden fur and sparkling green eyes was running towards them.

"Goldie!" gasped Lily in delight.

That could only mean one thing.

"We're going to Friendship Forest!" exclaimed Jess.

Friendship Forest was Lily and Jess's shared secret. Whenever Goldie came to find them, she took them there. It was a magical land, a truly amazing place, where all the animals could talk and lived in adorable little houses! The girls never had to worry about their parents wondering where they were, as time stopped still at home while they visited their magic animal friends.

Goldie usually purred and rubbed against their legs when she met them. But today she just gave an anxious meow and turned away, scampering down towards

Brightley Stream.

"Goldie seems worried," said Jess.

"She must need our help," agreed
Lily. "I hope there's nothing wrong in
Friendship Forest!"

The two friends dashed after Goldie.
She led them across the stream and into
Brightley Meadow on the other side.
Lily and Jess knew just where they were
going – straight to the old oak tree in the
middle of the field. The Friendship Tree!
It looked dead, but as they drew near, it
sprang into life. The bare branches were
suddenly covered in gold, red and orange

leaves. At once the air was filled with
song. Bluebirds and robins were swooping
down to feast on the juicy scarlet berries
hanging there.

Lily held Jess's hand. Together they read
aloud the two words that had sprung up
on the tree bark – "Friendship Forest!"

A door with a leaf-shaped handle
appeared. Jess opened it and Goldie
bounded through into the warm light that
spilled out from inside. The girls stepped
through after her. They felt tingly all over,
and knew this meant they were shrinking
a little.

As the magical light faded, they found
themselves in a sunny forest clearing. The
air was filled with the honey-and-lemon
scent of the flowers that grew all around.
Goldie was now standing on her back
legs, a golden scarf around her neck. The
friends ran to her and hugged her.

"Hello, girls!" she said.

"We're so happy to see you," said Lily.

"Is everything all right?" asked Jess.

Goldie shook her head. "I'd better let Ranger Tuftybeard explain."

A sturdy white goat with a neat beard stepped forward. He was wearing a knitted waistcoat and a cowboy hat and he had a pack on his back. The two friends had met the ranger on their last visit to Friendship Forest.

"I'm so pleased you girls are here," he said anxiously. "We need your help."

"Hello, Ranger Tuftybeard!" said Lily.

"What's wrong? Can we help?"

"Is Grizelda causing trouble again?" asked Jess.

Grizelda the witch was the only thing that ever spoiled Friendship Forest. She wanted to make the animals leave so she could have the forest all for herself. The girls had often helped Goldie to stop her.

 18

Ranger Tuftybeard nodded gravely. "I think Grizelda is up to her old tricks," he told them. "Only this morning I saw her orb floating over Magic Mountain again. It was near Fluffywhiskers Garden."

Magic Mountain was the place where all the magic of Friendship Forest came from. Without the crystals that were found there, every tree and plant would die and none of the girls' animal friends would be able to talk. There were four jobs to be done to create the magic that rained down over Friendship Forest, and four families, each in charge of one of the jobs.

On the girls' last visit to the forest, they'd met the Hoppytails, the family of rabbits who dug the crystals out of the mountain.

"I bet Grizelda and her trolls are planning another evil way to stop our friends making magic!" said Jess.

"Will you come back to Magic Mountain?" asked Goldie. "Will you help us protect the crystals?"

Lily and Jess didn't need to ask each other what their answer would be.

"Of course we will!" they cried.

CHAPTER TWO

Grizelda Strikes Again

"We'll take the train up the mountain,"
said Ranger Tuftybeard.

Lily and Jess grinned at each other.
They loved riding the Friendship Forest
train.

The ranger set off through the trees
with Goldie at his side. The girls hurried

after them, past charming little cottages
perched on branches and built into tree
trunks. They called a quick 'hello' to the
Fluffytails, as the squirrels scampered
along the branches with shopping baskets
in their paws.

Before long, Lily and Jess could see a
small green-and-yellow cabin. A sign on
it read 'Forest Halt'.

"There's the station," said Lily.

A smart, tomato-red steam train with a

golden stripe was sitting at the platform, sending puffs of squishy candyfloss into the air. In the driver's seat sat a fawn-coloured pug dog wearing huge goggles and a cap.

"Welcome back, Lily and Jess," he said, giving them a smart salute. "Hop on board."

"Hi, Mr Whistlenose," said the girls. They climbed into their carriage and sat down on the soft green-and-gold seats.

On the table between them was a plate of fairy cakes and some glasses of sparkly lemonade.

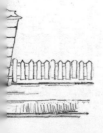

Goldie and Ranger Tuftybeard joined them. "Hold tight," called Mr Whistlenose. "We're in a hurry."

The train gave a cheerful toot and set off along the track.

Choof! Choof! Choof!

The girls looked out of the window as they tucked into their delicious iced treats. The forest was beautiful. The track ran beside a little stream where sunbeams sparkled on the water. Butterflies flitted

among bushes that were entwined
with sweet-smelling honeysuckle.

The train weaved its way up
Magic Mountain. The lower
slopes were lush with green
grass and sprinkled with daisies.
Above, the mountain was
covered in sparkling ice.
The peak was hidden in
fluffy white clouds.

Lily gasped as something appeared around her neck.

"My magic pendant," she said happily, holding out the beautiful white petal-shaped crystal that hung from a chain.

Pippa Hoppytail had given them each a magic crystal on their last visit to Magic Mountain. Lily's made things disappear, Jess's transformed things into something else, and Goldie's made things change colour.

"Mine's appeared too!' said Jess in delight. Her crystal was pink.

"They've all come back!" purred

Goldie, stroking her pretty blue jewel.
"But I hope we won't need them."

The train chugged its way past an
archway made of glittering stone.

"I remember that," said Lily. "It leads to
the Hoppytails' mine."

"And there they are!" said Jess eagerly.

Lily and Jess waved. Mum and Dad and

 27

all twelve little Hoppytails squeaked with excitement, Pippa loudest of all.

Mr Whistlenose brought the train to a halt at a wooden station. It was painted yellow, with baskets of primroses and violets hanging from silver hooks. Fragrant pink roses grew around the roof and chimney. A sign said 'Fluffywhiskers Garden'.

A beautiful garden stretched away into the distance. Blue streams wound round mossy green slopes, criss-crossed by charming stone bridges. The water flowed into sparkling ponds, with buttercups and

daisies growing on their banks.

"What a lovely place!" cried Jess as
they jumped down from their carriage.

"It is lovely," agreed Goldie. "We can't
let Grizelda and her trolls ruin it!"

"I must check that our other mountain families are safe," said Ranger Tuftybeard. He gave them a smile. "I'm sure the Fluffywhiskerses will be fine now you three are here." With that, the train set off. Lily and Jess waved until the last puffs of candyfloss steam were out of sight.

A short way down a garden path was a group of busy chipmunks.

"Are they the Fluffywhiskerses?" asked Lily, pointing.

They all had toffee-coloured fur with black and white stripes down their backs. They were scurrying around a big patch

of brown soil. Some were weeding, some
were planting vegetables and some were
pushing wheelbarrows up and down.
All around them were piles of crystals,
shimmering in the sunlight. The crystals
were the size of peas. Lily and Jess had
seen the Hoppytail family dig them up
from their mine.

 31

A young chipmunk wearing a pink
bobble hat was holding a shiny spade.
She puffed out her cheeks in a grin and
ran towards them. The girls bent down to
greet her.

"Hello, Lily and Jess," the
chipmunk said shyly. She
had a soft, fluffy tail and
bright black eyes. "I'm
Lola Fluffywhiskers. I
know all about you.
Come and meet my
family."

Clutching her spade, Lola scurried over

to the other chipmunks. She beckoned the girls to follow. They were introduced to Mr and Mrs Fluffywhiskers, and to Lola's three brothers.

"I'm Pickle," said the biggest one.

"I'm Tickle," said the middle one.

"And I'm Skip," said the smallest brother.

Lily and Jess said hello to them and then met Lola's aunties and uncles and all her cousins.

"Welcome to our garden," said Mrs Fluffywhiskers. "We're so glad Goldie's brought you here."

"Especially now Grizelda's been spotted," added Mr Fluffywhiskers.

The little animals all gave a shiver.

At the end of the line was an elderly chipmunk with crinkled whiskers and a soft knitted shawl around her shoulders. "This is Granny," said Lola.

"What do you think of our garden, girls?" asked Granny Fluffywhiskers, reaching up to grasp their hands

in a warm grip. "We grow magical fruit and vegetables, but our most important crop is the crystals."

"You plant the crystals here?" asked Lily.

"With the help of our magic spade," said Mr Fluffywhiskers.

Lily and Jess turned to look more closely at the spade Lola was holding, but she'd dropped it. Her eyes went wide and she dived into the nearest hole.

"What's the matter, Lola?" said Jess, worried.

Lily gave a gasp and pointed over Jess's

shoulder. "I think I know," she said in alarm. "Look!"

An orb of yellow-green light was shooting through the air, making straight for them.

"Oh no," whispered Jess. "Grizelda's coming!"

There was a loud CRACK and a shower of stinking yellow sparks. When they cleared, the evil witch stood there before them. Her long black cloak hung down her back, showing her knobbly elbows poking out of a purple tunic. Her long green hair whipped around her head

like lots
of angry
snakes.
The
Fluffywhiskers
family huddled
together, trembling. Lily, Jess
and Goldie stood in front of them.

"I might have known you meddlesome girls would be here," snapped Grizelda. "I don't know why you keep bothering to turn up. You'll never win against my powers."

"We've beaten you before," said Jess.

"And we'll beat you again."

"We won't let you hurt our friends!" declared Lily.

"Your silly animal friends won't be staying here once I've taken over the forest!" shrieked the witch. "I have a plan that cannot fail." She shuddered. "I feel sick when I think of the fluffy-wuffy magic in this place. I'm going to make sure that the forest is filled with my evil magic. And only my evil magic." She gave a piercing cackle of laughter.

Lily and Jess could hear frightened squeaks from the Fluffywhiskers family.

Grizelda suddenly grabbed Lola's spade from the ground.

Goldie gasped in horror. "Put that down," she said bravely.

But Grizelda took no notice. She held the spade up high above her head and shrieked a spell.

Magic, magic, take this spade

And hide it out of view

Then Magic Mountain will be mine

And Friendship Forest too.

The spade flew into the air, whirled around Grizelda's waving arms and vanished.

"My trolls will be guarding it now," she gloated. "You'll never find it. Ever!"

Her words echoed eerily through the garden. Screeching with delight, she wrapped her cloak round her.

There was a blinding flash and the nasty witch was gone.

CHAPTER THREE

Find the Spade!

The moment Grizelda had disappeared,
the Fluffywhiskers family gathered round
Goldie and the girls. They all wore
worried frowns. Lola crept out of her hole.
Her tiny tail drooped.

"I'm so sorry I ran away," she said,
hanging her head so her little knitted hat

 41

almost fell off.

Jess bent down to give the little
chipmunk a cuddle. "It's all right, Lola,"
she said gently. "Grizelda is very scary."

"How did you spot her orb before
any of us could see it?"
asked Lily. "That was
clever of you."

"It's because
Lola has really sharp
eyes," explained
Mr Fluffywhiskers
proudly. "The
sharpest eyes in

the whole of Friendship Forest!"

But Lola still looked ashamed. "I'm always the first one to spot danger," she said, "but I'm always the first one to run away too. And now that Grizelda has stolen the magic spade, we can't do our work to help the crystals grow."

"We can't let Grizelda get away with her wicked plan!' said Jess. She spotted an ordinary spade lying on the grass and picked it up. "Perhaps Lily and I can dig with this," she said. "We're bigger than you, so might manage it."

"And we're good at digging," said Lily.

Jess tried to push the spade into the earth. She felt as if she was trying to dig into solid rock.

"I don't understand," she said. "The soil looks soft enough."

"Thank you for trying," said Lola sadly. "But I'm afraid it's no good without the magic spade."

"The magic spade is the only one that can dig the earth in the special crystal patch," explained Granny Fluffywhiskers. She showed them a square of soil surrounded by dandyroses and pretty shells. "We plant the crystals here so they

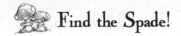

can grow big."

"But there won't be any more big crystals," wailed Lola. "And then there won't be enough magic. And then the forest will die."

"We still have one crystal growing,"

said Granny Fluffywhiskers, putting a paw round Lola's shoulders.

"I forgot," said Lola, brightening. "I planted a crystal here yesterday. You can just see its shoots."

Lily and Jess bent down over the crystal patch. Sure enough, tiny sparkling green leaves were poking through the earth.

Lola gave an excited squeak. "That means the crystal's nearly ready to be pulled out of the ground."

As the girls watched, a gleaming bud appeared on one of the shoots. It unfurled its petals to become a glittery pink flower.

"That's lovely," gasped Lily.

Lola pulled at the stem. A crystal began to appear. Slowly she pulled it free of the earth.

"That crystal is so beautiful, Lola!" said Jess.

"And it's very heavy," panted Lola as she struggled to pick it up. She gazed at the shining sides of the beautiful jewel. "But if I don't get the spade back, this is the last crystal we'll ever grow." Her black eyes filled with tears. "It will be the last crystal we pass on up the mountain to the next family. After that, all the magic in Friendship Forest will run out."

Lily scooped her up and gave her a warm cuddle.

"We won't let that happen," she said fiercely.

"We'll get the magical spade back," said Jess.

"We promise!" they said together.

Lola gazed from one to the other.
"Thank you," she said. "But first can you
help me carry this crystal home to our
cottage? We need to keep it safe."

"Of course," said Lily. She gently
took the crystal from Lola's paws. They
followed the little chipmunk down a
narrow, winding path bordered with
foxgloves and sunflowers. Her family
scampered along behind, carrying the
small crystals that had not yet
been planted.

They came to a small, grassy hill. It was
scattered with little doorways and tiny
round skylights.

"Your cottage is underground!"
exclaimed Jess. "It looks so cosy!"

Lily gave the crystal back to Lola as
the other chipmunks scampered inside,
putting the small crystals away where
they'd be safe.

"Thank you, Lily," said Lola.

"Now we must find the magic spade," declared Goldie.

"Grizelda said her trolls would be guarding it," said Jess thoughtfully. "If we can find the trolls, we can find the spade!"

Mrs Fluffywhiskers grasped the girls' hands in her furry paws. "That would be so kind of you," she said.

"And so brave," said Lola, with a wobble in her voice.

"I think you're brave enough to come with us, Lola," said Lily. "Do you think you could do it?"

 51

"Me?" gasped the little chipmunk.

"What a good idea," said Goldie. "Your sharp eyes would be very useful when we're hunting for the spade!"

"Will you help us?" asked Jess gently.

"Well ..." Lola looked unsure at first. Then she put her chin up bravely. "I'll do it," she said at last. "I'll help you find the magic spade."

CHAPTER FOUR

Sparkleberry Disaster!

"What do the trolls look like?" Lola asked.

Lily and Jess had seen the trolls last time they were here. They described the grey, knobbly creatures.

"Just like big rocks," Lily finished.

"I wonder where they could be,"

murmured Goldie, gazing around.

"Perhaps they're hiding in the rockery,"
said Lola shyly. "There are lots of rocks
among the flowers."

"That's brilliant, Lola," said Jess.
"They'd find it very easy to blend in
there."

The rockery was in a far corner of
the garden. Rocks had been arranged
in a pattern on a mound of earth with
pretty purple and white flowers growing
between them. Lemonbells made a
beautiful border around them. Their bells
tinkled in the gentle breeze.

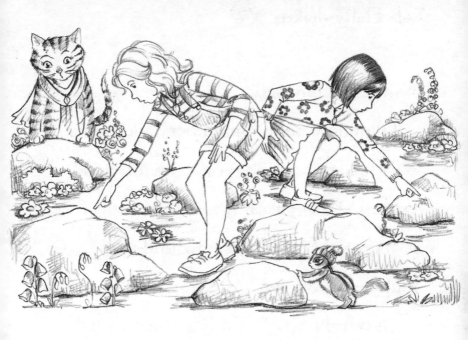

Everyone looked hard at the rocks.

"None of these look like trolls," said
Goldie.

"There's one way to find out," said
Jess boldly. She went up to the nearest
rock and gave it a prod. She got ready to
jump back in case it turned into a troll.

 55

Nothing happened.

Lily and Goldie joined her. Lola hung back. Then she took a deep breath and crept up to the nearest rock. She tapped it very gently with her paw and then scurried away.

"No trolls here," said Jess when they'd tested all the rocks in the rockery.

"Let's search the rest of the gardens," suggested Goldie.

They went over a bridge and came to a small fruit garden. A horrible sight met their eyes. Instead of neat rows of plants, there were only trampled stalks and stems.

"Oh no!" cried Lola. "Someone has taken all our sparkleberries!"

"Grizelda's trolls!" said Goldie, pointing out some big footprints in the soil.

"What are sparkleberries?" asked Jess.

"They're like strawberries," said Lola.

"But they're sparkly and they make your tongue fizzy. Magic Mountain is the only place where they grow."

"They're good for you," added Goldie.

Lola nodded. "They help to keep your fur shiny and your eyes bright. Sparkleberries are my number one favourite food." Lola frowned. "And now those nasty trolls have taken every one!"

Lily stared sadly at the ruined garden. Suddenly she gave a start. Two rocks behind a blackcurrant bush were moving. "I think we've found Grizelda's trolls," she whispered to the others.

The friends hid behind what Lola told them was a sunberry bush and watched as the two rocks grew long arms and hairy feet. Two heads popped up. Two sets of mean little eyes appeared on two ugly faces.

"I recognise those trolls," Lily told Lola. "That's Flinty. She's the one with the sticking-out ears."

"And that's Craggy, with the spiky white hair," added Goldie.

"They haven't got the spade," whispered Lola, "but they've got our sparkleberries!"

The trolls were carrying armfuls of shiny red berries. They both had red juice running down their knobbly chins.

"Dee-licious!" said Flinty in a gruff

voice. She stuffed a handful of berries into her mouth. "Om nom nom!"

"Om nom nom!" said Craggy, chewing loudly. "Scrum-dumptious!"

They grinned, showing rows of horrible gappy teeth.

"Those sparkleberries aren't yours!" shouted Lily, jumping out from their hiding spot.

"Give them back!" yelled Jess.

"Don't think so," giggled the trolls. Then they were off, zooming over a hump-backed bridge, through a cabbage patch, round a pond and into an orchard beyond.

They disappeared among the fruit trees.

The girls looked at Lola. The little chipmunk was trembling and trying to hide behind their legs. "Trolls are scary!" she squeaked.

Jess scooped her up. "We'll take care of you," she said, hugging her closely.

"Thank you," said Lola, peeking out from under her bobble hat. "I feel braver."

"We must go after the trolls," said Goldie. "Do you feel brave enough to come with us, Lola?"

Lola gulped. "I think so," she said in a tiny voice.

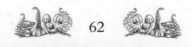

They raced across the garden. But when they reached the orchard, there was no sign of the trolls.

"They've disappeared!" said Goldie. "Which way should we go now?"

To their surprise, Lola jumped out of Jess's arms and trotted a little way in among the trees. "They've left a trail!" she said in excitement.

Everyone looked. Lola was right. Her sharp eyes had seen a line of dropped sparkleberries on the ground!

"Well spotted, Lola!" said Lily. "This will lead us straight to them!"

The four friends set off to follow the
trail again. They crept round the tree
trunks, ducking under branches that were

heavy with golden apples and juicy-
looking plums. They had just reached a

64

Sparkleberry Disaster!

grove of moonfruit trees when the trail

suddenly stopped.

"How strange," muttered Lily.

"Can you see them, Lola?" asked Jess.

Lola peered hard among the trees. Then

she shook her head. "There's no sign of them at all ... Eeek!" Lola squeaked as she, Goldie and the girls were all whisked off their feet!

CHAPTER FIVE

Captured!

They found themselves caught in a huge
net made of strong, thick vines. The net
tumbled them round and round in the
air. They caught glimpses of the ground
below them. The flowers and grass looked
a very long way away!

"What's happening?" cried Lola.

"We're caught in a trap," said Lily. She tugged at the woven green vines that had captured them. "I bet the trolls set it," said Goldie, trying to keep Lola safe in her arms. "That's why they left us a trail of sparkleberries."

The four friends struggled to get free but they just found themselves more tangled.

"This isn't working," said Jess. "But what if we use our pendants?"

"Of course!" said Lily. "I can use mine to make the net disappear!"

"Wait a minute, Lily," said Goldie anxiously. "We're a long way up. I'm sure to land on my paws but it's too far for you three to fall."

"What about using my pendant instead?" said Jess. "I can transform the net into something else the same shape."

"That's a good plan," said Goldie. "But transform it into what?"

Jess thought hard for a moment. "I know!" she said. "I'll turn it into a huge parachute. Then we'll all float gently down."

"Hurray!" squeaked Lola.

Jess felt for the pendant around her neck. It wasn't there!

"My pendant's gone," she told the others.

"So is mine," gasped Lily.

"And mine," said

Goldie. "What's happened to them?"

"I can see them!" said Lola. "They're on the ground. They must have fallen off when the net grabbed us."

Lily peered down, but all she could see were tiny shapes in the grass. "Your eyesight is amazing, Lola!" she exclaimed.

"How are we going to get them back?" asked Jess. She pulled at the vines, trying to make a bigger gap between them. But they didn't move.

Lola began to wriggle beside her. "I can get my head through," said the little chipmunk. She wriggled some more. "And

my front paws. I think I'm small enough
to get out! I could climb down and get
the pendants."

"Be careful!" said Lily.

Lola gave a nod. Then she scrabbled
at the net again. "I'm going," she
announced.

They watched as she squeezed between
the vines on to a nearby tree branch. She
crept carefully towards the trunk. Then
she froze.

"What's wrong?" asked Jess.

"I'm scared," whispered Lola. "Those
horrible trolls might come back to check

their trap and find me!"

"It's all right to be scared," said Goldie, soothingly. "It was very brave of you to try."

"Come back, Lola," said Lily. "We'll think of something else."

But then Lola gave a sudden swish of her tail. Her bright eyes looked all around. "No trolls in sight!" she declared. "I'm doing it!"

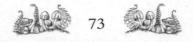

"Go, Lola!" whispered Lily and Jess together.

In a twinkling, Lola had scrambled down the trunk to the ground. She looked again in every direction, her nose twitching.

She picked up the three pendants from the grass. They filled her paws.

"How will you manage to climb back up?" called Goldie in alarm.

"Easy peasy," Lola called back. She looped the pendants round her neck and waved her empty paws at them.

The little chipmunk headed back up

the tree. But the
pendants were very
big and heavy. Lily
and Jess gasped as
Lola's claws scrabbled at
the bark. They could see
she was panting with the
effort.

"You can do it,
Lola!" urged Jess.

"Cling on to
that knot in the
trunk!" called Lily.

"Good idea,"

said Goldie. "Lola can have a rest there."

Lola got her breath back. Then she
set off again. Slowly she inched her way
up on to the branch above the girls and
Goldie. Suddenly she slipped. Her paws
reached desperately for a hold.

"Lola!" cried Jess.

For a moment they thought the heavy
pendants were going to drag her off the

branch. But Lola just clenched her jaw
and continued. She wrapped her tail
round the branch.

"Don't worry," she said. "I'm safe."

She dangled upside down above the net.
Then she jumped on to it and squeezed
back through a gap. She was out of
breath but her eyes were full of delight.

"I did it," she panted.

Lily and Jess cheered. "Well done!"

Goldie helped Lola to take the
pendants from around her neck. Jess took
hers in her hand.

"Here we go," she said. "I'm going to

turn the net into a parachute. Hold on tight!"

They each grasped a vine and held it firmly.

Jess chanted the magic words. "Crystal flower, show your power!"

CHAPTER SIX

Yuckleberries

Whoosh! In an instant, the net turned into a silky pink parachute. Lily, Jess, Goldie and Lola all found they were each holding a long ribbon. The ribbons tied themselves gently round their hands. With the help of the parachute, they floated slowly down to the ground. Just as their

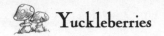

toes touched the grass, the silky material changed back into a tangle of vines again.

"We've made it!" said Lily.

"But we have to watch out for the trolls," said Jess.

"Can you see them, Lola?" asked Goldie.

But Lola didn't answer. She was gazing at something in the distance. "That's strange," she said.

"What's the matter?" asked Jess.

"That tree over there," said the little chipmunk. She pointed to a thin, spindly tree growing by some primroses. "It must be new. I've never noticed it before."

"It's not the same as the others," said Goldie.

"I know what it is!' exclaimed Lola, suddenly jumping in excitement. "It's the magic spade. I'd recognise it anywhere!"

Lola was right. The spade had been stuck in the ground and the handle covered with a few twigs and leaves.

"The trolls must have tried to hide it," said Jess.

"Well, they didn't do a very good job!" said Lily, marching towards the magic

spade. "We'll soon get it
back."

But Jess caught her
arm and pointed. Two
trolls were crouching
behind a bush next to a big pile of
sparkleberries.

"Oh no!" whispered Goldie. "It's
Craggy and Flinty! How are we going to
get to the spade now?"

"We can't let them see us," Lily
whispered back. "This way."

Everyone followed her to the safety of
a broad tree trunk. They peered out at the

trolls. Craggy and Flinty were slurping loudly and pushing great handfuls of the stolen fruit into their mouths.

"We have to lure them away from the spade," said Goldie.

"Food is all they care about," said Jess. "But they've still got plenty of sparkleberries left."

"I've got it!" said Lily. "Goldie, your pendant can make things change colour. You could make the sparkleberries look nasty. Then they won't want to eat them any more."

"They'll have to go off and find

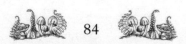

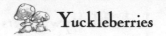

something else to fill their greedy bellies!"
said Goldie.

Goldie held her
pendant tightly in
her paw and said
the magic words,
"Crystal flower,
show your power!"

Pfff! Every berry immediately turned
from mouth-watering red to yucky
yellow with murky green spots.

Flinty stared at the berry in her gnarled
hand. She spat out her mouthful. "Bleeh!"
she growled. "Horrible!"

Craggy threw his sparkleberries to the ground. "Not sparkleberries, yuckleberries! Got to find scrummy food."

"Something yummy for my tummy!" said Flinty, nodding her big rocky head.

The two grumbling trolls jumped to their feet. A second later, they'd raced off through the orchard.

"It worked!" cried Goldie.

But just as they were going to rescue the spade, two more trolls came lumbering into view.

"Oh, no," said Lily. "Now how can we get the spade?"

CHAPTER SEVEN

Tricked Trolls

A troll with shaggy grey hair was
stomping round and round the spade.
Another one was right behind him,
swinging her long arms.

"It's Rocky and Pebble!" said Goldie.
"We should've known they'd be nearby."

The trolls were muttering to themselves

as they went.

"Stupid Craggy, stupid Flinty," grumbled Rocky.

"Grizelda be cross," added Pebble. She wiped her wobbly nose with her big hairy hand.

"We guard spade," said Rocky. "We good trolls."

"What do we do now?" whispered Lola. Her whiskers twitched anxiously and the girls could see her paws were trembling. "They're very big and scary."

"I think I know," said Lily, her eyes lighting up. "I'll use my pendant and

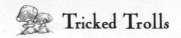

make the spade disappear." She took the stone in her hand and said the magic words. "Crystal flower, show your power!"

Ping! The magic spade vanished.

Rocky gave a roar. "Where spade go?"

"Pebble not know," shouted Pebble,

waving her long arms like a windmill.

"Rocky and Pebble get spade!" cried Rocky.

They lumbered away, poking their big noses under bushes and into trees. At last they were out of sight.

Lily let her crystal go, and the magic spade reappeared.

The girls, Goldie and Lola all hugged in celebration.

Lola scampered over and pulled the spade from the ground. Together they ran back to the Fluffywhiskerses' house.

The chipmunks were so pleased to see them that they skipped round Lily and Jess, squeaking with delight.

"Thank you," they chorused. "You've

saved our magic spade!"

"And the magic of Friendship Forest!" said Mrs Fluffywhiskers. "We'll be able to plant the little crystals now."

"Let's celebrate first," said Granny Fluffywhiskers.

"A splendid idea," said Lola's father. "But we'd better hide the spade in case Grizelda comes back."

He took the spade and hurried back to the cottage.

Granny Fluffywhiskers puffed out her cheeks. "Time for fun," she announced. "What shall we play?"

 91

Lola's brothers all chirped at once. "Let's play tag!"

"I'm it!" shouted Mr Fluffywhiskers, and he ran round laughing as he tried to catch all the young chipmunks.

The afternoon whizzed by as they played and had fun races all around the flowerbeds.

"Juice time," called Granny Fluffywhiskers at last. She had a jug of bright red drink and glasses on a tray.

"Sparkleberry juice!" squeaked Lola.

"Just the thing for a warm afternoon," said Goldie.

Lily and Jess took a glass each.

"It's delicious!" they said together.

"It tastes of strawberries," said Jess.

"It's sending fizzes up my nose," laughed Lily. "We've had a lovely time with your family, Lola."

"It has been lovely, hasn't it?" said Lola. Her eyes suddenly widened. "Look out!" she cried, pointing across the garden.

A yellow-green orb was hurtling towards them.

"Oh no! It's Grizelda," cried Goldie. "She's back."

CHAPTER EIGHT

Brave Lola!

Craack! Grizelda appeared in an explosion of stinking yellow sparks.

Lily and Jess stood together, facing the witch. The Fluffywhiskers family scurried behind them. Jess looked down in surprise. There was one little chipmunk who hadn't run to hide.

Lola stood bravely between her and Lily. She was glaring up at Grizelda.

"I know you've got the magic spade back," snapped the witch. "You tricked my trolls. But you won't trick me. I want it now!" She swished her cloak as her mean eyes searched round. "Where is it?"

"Not telling you," said Lola. She put her paws on her hips and stared fearlessly up at Grizelda. "We'll never stop making magic to keep Friendship Forest safe. Ever!"

"And we'll always come to help our friends," declared Lily.

"That's right," said Jess. "We love Friendship Forest. So hands off, Grizelda!"

Grizelda turned purple with rage. "Stupid girls!" she shrieked, her eyes blazing. "You miserable creatures! You won't get away with this. I'll be back!"

With that, she disappeared in a spray of smelly sparks.

The Fluffywhiskers family rushed out

from their hiding places.

"Hurrah for Lola!" cried Granny.
"You're a brave girl."

"And hurrah for Lily, Jess and Goldie,"
called Mr Fluffywhiskers.

"Good riddance to Grizelda!" squeaked
Lola's brothers.

Lola suddenly jumped up and down
in excitement. "Look!" she cried. "Look!
Ranger Tuftybeard is here."

Lily and Jess followed her pointing paw.
But although they stared hard, no one
could spot the ranger.

"Your eyes are so sharp!" said Goldie.

"Where is he?"

"He's in the train!" squeaked Lola. "It's coming down the mountain. He'll be so pleased to know that we've stopped Grizelda's wicked plan."

At last the others could see him too. Ranger Tuftybeard was waving to them from the little mountain train that was pulling into the station. Everyone rushed to meet him.

"I've come back to check that you're all OK," he said.

"We are," said Goldie with a smile. "The crystals are safe, thanks to Lily and

 99

Jess — and brave little Lola."

They told Ranger Tuftybeard how they'd defeated the trolls and got the spade back.

"We showed Grizelda she can't bully us," finished Lola fiercely. "I'm not scared of her any more."

"Your family must be very proud of you, Lola," said Ranger Tuftybeard,

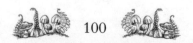

giving her a big smile.

"We are," said Mrs Fluffywhiskers.

"You are a hero, Lola," said Jess, bending down to give her a kiss on her soft cheek. "We couldn't have got the spade back without you and your sharp eyes."

"And I wouldn't have been brave enough without you and Lily," said Lola.

Lily smiled. "But now it's time for us to go home," she said. "Although we'll be back whenever you need us."

Lily, Jess and Goldie got on board the train. The Fluffywhiskers family stood in

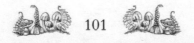

a line with Ranger Tuftybeard and waved
as the train pulled away.

~

When they reached the Friendship Tree,
the girls gave Goldie a big hug.

"Thank you, Lily and Jess," said Goldie,
her green eyes shining. "I don't know
what we'd do without you both."

"You can count on us," said Lily. "We'll
never let Grizelda take this lovely forest."

Goldie touched the bark of the tree.
The door swung open and golden light
flooded out. The girls stepped through
into the light. They felt the usual tingles

as they returned to normal size and found themselves back in Brightley Meadow.

They walked back across the stream. When they got back to Helping Paw, Jess stopped and crouched beside the pile of leaves they'd made.

"The leaves are moving again," she whispered.

"I wonder why," said Lily.

A tiny pink nose suddenly pushed its way out of the pile. Two beady eyes looked at them them.

"It's a baby hedgehog!" exclaimed Jess.

The leaves moved again. Now the girls

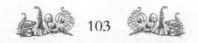

could see four more sweet little babies.

"There's a whole family of them hiding in the leaves!" said Lily softly.

"Perhaps they're playing hide and seek," said Jess. "Just like the Fluffywhiskers family!"

The bold baby hedgehog was staring at them with unblinking eyes.

Lily and Jess smiled at each other. They knew another brave creature who kept an eye on things – their good friend Lola Fluffywhiskers!

The End

Wicked witch Grizelda is still trying to ruin the magic of Friendship Forest. Can little goat kid Emma Littleleap help save the day?

Find out in Lily and Jess's next adventure,

Emma Littleleap Takes a Chance

Turn over for a sneak peek ...

"There! That's the last bit done." With a swish of her paintbrush, Lily Hart put the final touches to the words on the sign:

HELPING PAW WILDLIFE HOSPITAL

Her best friend, Jess Forester, had painted lots of little animals around the edge. Both girls adored animals and loved to help out at the wildlife hospital, which Lily's parents ran in a barn at the bottom of their garden.

"Now the sign looks lovely and new again," Jess said.

The girls admired each other's

handiwork as Jess's tabby kitten, Pixie, nuzzled their legs.

Lily picked up the kitten. "Look, Pixie!" She laughed. "It's like a typical day in Friendship Forest!"

Jess grinned. Friendship Forest was their secret – a magical place where animals lived in little cottages and could talk! The girls' special friend, Goldie the cat, often came to take them there, and together the three of them had had some amazing adventures. The girls always enjoyed meeting their friends at the Toadstool Café, boating down Willowtree River or having a sleepover with Goldie in her grotto.

When Pixie started to squirm in Lily's arms, she gently put the kitten down. She watched as Pixie chased a butterfly behind a rose bush. Lily turned back to Jess, who frowned at the sign. "Something's missing," said Jess.

Lily put her head to one side. "Mmm. It's that empty space below the words. What could go there?"

Suddenly, soft fur brushed against Jess's leg, and she glanced down. A beautiful golden cat with emerald green eyes gazed at her.

"Goldie!" Jess bent down to stroke her and the cat cuddled up in her arms.

"She's come to take us to Friendship Forest!" said Lily. "We're off on another adventure!"

Read

Emma Littleleap Takes a Chance

to find out what happens next!

Lily and Jess love lots of different animals –
both in Friendship Forest
and in the real world.

Here are their top facts about

CHIPMUNKS
like Lola Fluffywhiskers:

- Although extremely cute, chipmunks are considered to be rodents and pests.

- Lola is a Palmer's chipmunk. This is the most endangered species of chipmunk in the world.

- Chipmunks talk to each other a lot, using bird-like noises and gestures like sign language as a way of communicating with one another.

- Chipmunks have pouches in their cheeks so they can store food until they return to their burrow. When full, their pouches can expand to three times larger than their head.

- A group of chipmunks is called a 'scurry'.

Magic
Animal Friends
Can you keep the secret?

There's lots of fun for everyone at
www.magicanimalfriends.com

Play games and explore the secret world of
Friendship Forest, where animals can talk!

Join the
Magic Animal Friends Club!

→✕ Special competitions →✕
→✕ Exclusive content →✕
→✕ All the latest Magic Animal Friends news! →✕

To join the Club, simply go to

www.magicanimalfriends.com/join-our-club/